# Daniel's New Home

**by Christine Keighery**
**illustrated by Chantal Stewart**

## Table of Contents

# Chapter I
## Leaving Home

When Dad came in from the fields today, Cara was crying.

"She's hungry," said Mam. I was hungry, too. But I wasn't crying. I am seven years old plus two whole months, so I have to help.

Dad gave Cara a cuddle and she stopped howling. Soon, we will have another baby.

I really want a brother.

"How are the potatoes?" asked Mam. I held my breath.

"The potatoes are ruined," said Dad. "We cannot eat or sell them." When I let my breath out, it sounded like a sigh.

"We have to leave Ireland," said Mam. "We have a family to look after, and not enough food."

"We should go to North America like the Sullivans," said Dad.

I thought of how Fergus Sullivan always bragged about going to America. Then we never heard from him after he went across the Atlantic Ocean!

"Your Uncle Paddy will help us get settled there," said Dad.

Uncle Paddy is my favorite uncle. If he was brave enough to go to America, I can be brave, too.

I sat on Grandma's lap, even though I'm too big for sitting on knees. I held her wrinkled hands.

"Dad said we'll have to be patient," I told Grandma. "The boat trip to America will take a long time."

Grandma smiled. "Darling," she said, "you will have to be patient without me. I want to stay here. But I might come when you are settled."

# Chapter 2
# On the Boat

*October 20, 1847*

We are on a huge boat, headed for America. There are more than 200 people on board. It is very crowded!

Everyone is excited. But when the sea is rough, Mam feels sick. It is hard to find a soft space for her to lie down.

# Chapter 3
# A New Home

Finally, we have arrived in America. We are staying with Uncle Paddy. Dad is working on the railways. I am proud of him. He is so strong.

I don't know any children here. I play marbles by myself. Today a marble rolled back to me. When I looked up, it was Fergus Sullivan!

"I see you've practiced, Daniel," he said.

## Chapter 4
# A New Baby

I came back home today. I was staying at Uncle Paddy's house because Mam was having a baby.

Uncle Paddy said the baby will be an American! I can't wait to meet my new sister.

"Annie looks just like you, Daniel," said Mam. I held out my finger, and my baby sister grabbed it.

"Do you know she is an American?" I said.

# Comprehension Check

## Retell the Story

Use a Prediction Chart
and the pictures to help
you retell this story.

| What I Predict | What Happens |
|---|---|
|  |  |
|  |  |
|  |  |

## Think and Compare

1. Turn to page 7. What makes you think that Daniel will feel safe in America? *(Make and Confirm Predictions)*

2. How might you feel if you had to live in a different country? *(Apply)*

3. What are some of the reasons people move from one country to another? *(Analyze)*